What a waste.

Introduction

Why I wrote this is a secret.
A petty and selfish secret according to my current views about myself. It should be obvious that I really won't tell you why I want to publish this book.

Nonetheless, I have realised that I can act in innumerable ways that end up with me not being upto somebody's expectations. I hardly have an understanding of how humans work. More to it, I hardly have a clue about how I work.

I'm a stimulant-fueled mediocre human who claims to practise art but is just distracting himself from the misdeeds conducted in the past that don't seem to be comforting enough to have a standalone conversation with. So I attempt to mute the past with the thoughts of being noticed as someone far more than who can be associated back to the consequences of one's actions. That's why I write sometimes, which is not the secret.

The distracting thought of helping someone out of this book while I so foreseeably drivel down the abyss of questions about morals, the deserving and the undeserving, the good, the bad, the unfathomable destruction and all the many more complexities that the nature of the world and the mind offers is not a secret either. But I guess this book does end with a proposal.

It's a sad fact that I have to let it be clear that whatever destructive inclinations this book has offered about society, people, relations, and self is a mere character and a result of what this environment itself has helped create. The proposal that this book has to offer is to consider a possibility to break the chains of self doubt and to paint a bigger picture out of this character.

I find it my duty to put forth an image where a character so oblivious to its surroundings is gifted with the awareness of destructive abilities and the after effects that could be. Only then, it becomes a question about what we choose to become.

What a waste.

Harshil Dhameja

The birthmark on your
Shoulder ignites me.
It reminds me
Of the child that was inside me
It ignites me.
The memory fights me
The vision terrifies me
The birthmark on your
Shoulder
It shines on you
&
It blinds me.

Dead roses in my room
They are still in the water
A sense of false hope.
The mind cannot rest, it cannot cope
Music in the background to save me from the
demon
But the batteries will die and the demon will devour
me. It'll eat me and shit me out.
I'll be nothing but a dead rose in a room
Still kept in water.
A dead rose kept in water. That's prison.
This false sense of hope is prison.
Punishment is freedom.
And I am still a dead rose, trying to hang on to the
water.

Three words,
'I dont know'
These, are meditation.
A way of life, a way to control my impulsive
thoughts.
These, matter to me.
Or do they?
I dont know.
Does anything matter?
I dont know.
Uncertainty might be a blessing, or it might be a
curse.
All I know is that change is constant
But, I dont know.

Note to self:
Be what you expect from the world. Expect forgiveness? Be forgiving. Expect love? Know how to. Have the courage to forgive the unforgivable.
If you believe that even one person in the world will accept good change, be that person yourself. Resentment is natural. But so can love be.

I carried her scent to sleep. Lucky to have a day when someone else sits around you. We never touched but I still carried her scent wherever I went. Some, I still do.
Even these gifts from the world are temporary. I wish we meet again.

Sublime.
This pain, this crime,
This detachment is sublime.
It's fun.
This prison of the mind,
The hunger, the suffering,
The rush, the chase,
The rejection, the hate,
The depreciation, the smoke,
The torture, the breathlessness,
All sublime.

To love the world that kicks you a thousand times, and a thousand more, is power.
Absolute, undefeated, infinite power. Forgive all there is. Tomorrow you won't be able to. The world will kick you down as it should, but there is divine beyond that. Your presence as nature has planned. And all that is special today, is only as long as it lasts.
REMEMBER
Death. Genuine empathy. Gratitude. The power of the universe to punish you, and the nothingness of it. The nothingness of popularity, likability, pleasure, pain and most importantly, the nothingness of you.

Those ten seconds, I was happy. Satisfied. In the present.
The craving of that touch, the need for comfort and the chase. The hopeless romance and the uncertainty of all of it.
Those then seconds.
The mindfuck.
The comfort.

The obscure pain of wanting people to like me, is, well, painful. But then, it's just the addictive kind of sad. Give up on the addictive kind of sad. Let's hope it heals. Everything heals.

The sun, the waves, the sand on which we walked
barefoot, the rocks that we jumped off, the concrete
walls that we climbed that day,
All of it was beautiful.
But the fact that 'we' did it, was unbelievable.
If there is a god, I pray to him sincerely, to heal me.
Give me peace and the strength to love what there is.
hope.

Insect

Eating away the membranes,
An insect walks inside my skull
Slowly gulping down my feelings all
Digesting then, excreting a fluid
Stimulates to find conflict.
'Fore I act the way not intended,
To find a fill for the crawlie
I forget what I came here for.
There are others who
Have theirs eaten too
Collapse nonetheless like me
Like turning into a zombie.
With hope we fight,
Until none of us is right.

I wish the kids sitting on the bench next to me, knew how hateable I could be. How hateable and miserable they could be if they did'nt realise what not to do. How the old uncles chatting on the other benches, taught forgiveness to every human out there, and how beautiful it would feel to be, loved. I wish all those who know me, know how fucked of a brain I have. How two minutes of happiness is followed by 23 hours and 58 minutes of self ridicule. Self hate and all this willingness to die and all the fucking hate and pain that I give to others.

I wish they'd also teach me how to be at peace, or atleast pursue it.

I wish, but would it all, or any of it, come true?

I just wish to die. I fail to understand the absence of punishment and the constant presence of regret that comes with it.

I fail to understand you, my parents, god, nature and all the significance they attach to each other.

All I understand is this addiction to misery.

I have become a truly pathetic person in my own mind. Scum. But, hope prevails I believe.

And I believe that a beautiful life, a life worth living, even after consuming all the hate possible, is there waiting for me patiently. It's waiting patiently to allow me to find what I love, and help me love it, in peace, in harmony with the misery, and in company of someone, who is a human of their own right.

I fear a lot. Fear is irrational, I know. But I can't accept.
I want that confidence back.
No one in society knows the good I have.
I don't either.
They, then, shouldn't know the bad either.
The urge to confess has to die.
I want that confidence back.
It's all in my mind. I am not my mind.
Its nothing but a little part of me.
A shaky little child.
I don't wanna live like this but I need the strength to live. To live on my own terms.
Im paranoid and afraid of punishment, of getting cancelled. Of jail. Of being the worst person in the world. Of getting worse.
I feel I don't deserve love either.
I cried in the arms of multiple people that day.
I want love. But I'm afraid. Afraid of losing love. Afraid that guilt might be the only thing I contain.
Maybe I'm right. Guilt might be the only thing I have.
But I want to live peacefully, without fear. Fear of being hated by the world. Why do I think about the opinions of others? I'm scared that I will reveal my demons and that would ruin everything, atleast everything around me.
I want to lose that ego.
Let the world bash me.
Would it even matter if they did? That is society, They hate.

I need a break. I have convinced myself that all I have done is wrong.

I cannot confess. I cannot apologise. I don't know what to do.

I need to be fearless enough to love. I want to.

If I commit a crime, I need the strength to face the consequences. I need the strength to accept that the world might not care enough. I need the strength to live with myself, with my music. Need the strength to not judge myself, simply for my wrongs.

I need to focus on the 95 things I've done right and the 5 things I've done wrong, in that ratio.

To understand how to forgive. Others and myself. To not be afraid to live unproductive, chill, pressure free, without result.

To feel the grass under my legs. To look up at the sky and just feel the unprecedented range it has.

To meditate.

To be wrong.

To not confess.

To face it if I do.

To answer to no one.

No one knows my story but me. Not my family. Not my friends. No one else. They are just a character. They dont know what I have, what I want and I don't get to decide if they deserve to know. I don't know what I deserve and don't know what I will get.

I get what I get. If its pain, misery, hunger, crime, jail, impatience, cruelty, love, care, cancer, hate, peace. All of it.

The world hates if it has to, I am the one who has
to be fearless.
Forever.
I want gratitude and the strength to live with the
lack of, if necessary. Punishment and the
strength to live with the lack of.

Is that too much to ask?
Don't know.
Need the strength to not know.
To also understand that I know some things. To
know the world is unfair. I am too.

To enjoy wanting normal things.
A girlfriend, wife, kid,car, books, something to
care about and look after.
Home.
I want a home.
I don't know.
I want peace and the strength to keep it.
I pray to whatever there is.

A kid, I was a kid who could love his parents, his ancestors; i had that compassion.

There was a time, that kid would sit on the stomach of his grandmother, tickle her until she was out of breath, yet she never got angry.

He would punch her chest and her stomach, ride her legs and pretend to be an aeroplane. They would look out the window at midnight and listen to the few awake birds.

Now the kid has grown up.

But this is not about the kid this time.

She has grown old too. She rarely gets to meet her grandchild that she dearly loved. This love was taken away by the unlucky people who didn't understand love. I feel pity for them and for the kid.

Now her skin is hanging inches below her bones. It's red in parts and flaky all the way. She cannot talk and barely moves. All she can do is smile when the name of the kid pops up. Smile and look at that kid and reminisce about whatever that is left inside of her mysterious brain. That will go away too.

What love would be left then?

There are patches on her skin that are more red and flaky than others. How did she end up going through that pain?

What hate do people contain?

How does love diminish into nothingness,
everytime?
Did she deserve this hate?
Did she deserve this pain?
Did she not?
Do we get to decide?
Do we get to decide who deserves peace?
I don't know.

I wish I had the bravery to tell her how beautiful she looks. But then again, I wish a lot.

25-09-23

Sleep deprived, Every night I lose myself to the thoughts of self sabotage. I've found comfort here.
Someone pull me out.
Because apparently, I have no strength of my own.
This book was a gift too.
I need another.

25-09-23

This book found it's end. Im glad I wrote good things in here.
Eventually, I hope, there will be something i'm good at.
Maybe writing. Maybe some other form of art.

Things are killing me right now but there is nature and the sound of birds keeping me sane.
Some uncle cutting the grass. What life must he have led?

Hasn't he been bad?
Has he lived an honest life?
A million dumb questions pop up in my head and
I find the answers not comfortable enough.
Being human is tough.
Hope is a good thing said dufsrene. Maybe the
best of the things. And no good thing ever dies.
Smoke up. Sober up. Smile. Charm. Off we go.
Off we go.

Daydreaming

I don't want to be fascinated by the riches, the american dream, the boulevards, the rock and roll tickets which cost a thousand bucks for mixing our sweats and sharing puffs of weed with strangers…

I want to talk and walk and get robbed with the rats of the underground, hated by each in sight yet working for their own right. The riches are too predictable, and I live under their roof. I'm too predictable.

The people down there, whose name only their closest ones know, are doing jobs, tricking, robbing, shooting; are far more interesting than this person typing on a shitton worth of a laptop that he begged from his parents.

I'm addicted to these headphones and this constant bragging of a lifestyle which shows nothing of me, but what I want others to see me as.

And, I'm tired as well, turning apathetic to things which I should have invested my interests in.

Now, I don't know what I want to be and what they want me to be.

Neither makes any difference to me, for I have juggled and failed both of them quite consistently.

Well, there we go. A new cool book. A book of dreams and the failure. Ambitions and the failure. Love and the lack of. Hope.

27-09-23

Let me unlearn
The wrong I have done.
Bring me back to life
This is not it. I feel guilt and shame. Pure.
Will there be someone out there?
Bring me back to life I say. This philosophy is not worth it.
Oh lord, get me to that child or let me have a new life.
I pray for that valley. I pray for Kangra.
If I'm nowhere, you'll find me there.

I pray for Kangra

That boy doesn't know what's there. All he knows is that he wants a silent escape. Temporary. Painful. But better, probably.

'Lets find out' he whispers. 'But kill me if I don't wanna know what lies in there'

He buys the ticket. And with three pairs of clothes, a watch, a knife, a bag, a book and some cash; jumps on the train. Not looking behind he whispers to himself,

'Kangra, take me home. I pray'

27-09-23

With guilt, with shame, I don't feel anything. Let me feel pain. If that's a feeling, it's still something. Then, pain is proof that I'm alive. And to be alive is to be human. I hope.

I have always written about hope. But one part of me is ever increasing in size since a long time now.

The so called 'demon'. Humans name their imperfections demons. In my head that imperfection is getting bigger and bigger, everyday.

Hope is false; I have started to believe like that. Sometimes I wonder if hope is true. Our parents, girlfriends, friends, children, wives, teachers and all the others bring us up with the foundation of hope. They fill us with hope. And now it feels like a virus installed in me. I don't know how to write what I'm feeling.

There is a part of me who is always sorry for others, but there is also a very real part of me that wants to watch the world burn. I want you all to go through, what goes through my head. Real event OCD.

People, constantly passing judgement. I have become a zombie. Every night the suicidal ideations become stronger. Every day is like a bonus.

I should've been dead yesterday. But since I'm not, today sucks just as much.

Every passing minute, I get uglier and uglier. The thoughts get uglier. You get uglier. I'm not going back, no. I'm destroying everything beautiful about the world that I created. I have no control over this destruction and now I have started to find comfort in this destruction. That is sad.

It will get bleaker and bleaker every second. First there will be hope, then there will be judgement. Then ridicule. Then hate. Then it will be nothing. The hope will turn into nothing. Your ugly body, your ugly words, actions, you yourself will be forgotten. But before that, you will be hated by each individual that you wanted not to hate you.

Tell me then, why would suicide be worse? Why is being a zombie worse? Atleast then, you're only killing the world around you and not letting others have the opportunity to ridicule.

People never understand, some of them pretend to. Most just ridicule. Even the strongest, most powerful ones are the insecure ones. Let me die in peace I say. Atleast let me die in peace.

Everything around me sucks. Everything that revolves around me sucks. I suck. I will disappear completely. Losing my shit. I lose. I lose. The light goes dimmer and dimmer. The shadows win. I lose. Like I was even light someday. I will be forgotten. There is no comfort in living. The mind feels heavy. The blank book had more freedom. I don't know I'm just rambling at this point.

I want to kill that hope. I want everyone to be hopeless. Everything sucks. You all suck just as much as I do. Which is a lot. Is there something more to it than this? Really this? If this is it, then kill me please.

Be hopeless. Don't be hopeless. But if you are one, it's not wrong. Make hopeless art. The world has destroyed itself anyways. Make hopeless art. Make art.

OCD OCD OCD OCD OCD OCD OCD OCD past past past past past. Enough. Not enough yet. A lot more to go. OCD. OCD. OCD. PAST. HATE. SHIT. OCD. Hate. narcissistic. Fuck. Fuck. Kill me. Hurt me. Fuck me.

Hide your insecurities. Show your insecurities. Treat them nicely. Don't treat them nicely. Kill them all. Kill yourself. Don't care. Care. Its all shit to me. Lose everything. Be everything. Make hopeless art. Be hopeless. Stay hopeless. Spread hopelessness. Spread despair. Fuck life.

Drain me out of my senses. Then make me write some more. Then more. Im 22 and I'm hopeless and I'm rambling. I have hope, false hope, that something good will come out if I keep on rambling. But nothing will. Things never work out as we intend to. We all suck as humans and we shall all be killed soon.

Make hopeless art. Make art. Make my art. Make art. You suck. Art sucks. Aesthetics suck. We all suck. I'm turning into a misanthrope. I hate myself more than I hate humans. But I hate humans too.

The music is comfort. I feel every beat. It runs through my blood. Only the music makes sense. It will also not, after some time. Man, philosophy sucks. Philosophy sucks. Shit sucks.

11-10-23

Lose everything. Lose art. Lose hope. Lose all the pain. Lose all the guilt. Lose the right and the wrong for a moment. Lose your judgement. Lose morals. Lose yourself. Lose everything you hate and everything you cherish.

Then sit beside me and listen to the music of nature. The kingfisher feathers. The caterpillars eating away the leaves. Watch the tree grow older and older every second. Watch it grow new leaves. Watch it decay. Watch death. Then be death. All beside me.

Me not doing anything destroys a lot of things. Me doing things destroys too. Me trying to solve something destroys too. Me thinking, destroys too. Am I going somewhere with this? Nope. Destruction is inevitable and fucks shall not be given I guess.

To give up at this point almost feels criminal. Maybe I am a criminal then. Maybe I'm not. Suicide wasn't an option. Now it has become a choice. I dont know what to write. Maybe I'll write about not knowing. Ah, this sucks. Everything sucks. I'm a pussy. I cannot be an anarchist. I cannot be anything. FUCK THIS!

Don't have the quest to do something. Just keep learning. Keep failing. Don't try. Fuck this life and keep living. You can never be sure you're gonna have hope. So be hopeless. Stay hopeless. Don't try.

Destroy life. Let life destroy itself. Keep writing. Get bored. Write some more. Be hopeless. Don't write. Fuck things that don't matter. Fuck those that don't matter. Fuck those that DO matter. Let everything destroy itself. Letting go means letting go of hope. Hope is a fantasy. Let go of the fantasy. Don't chase. Just be. Don't even try to be. Just be. Accept the past. Let everything be. Let the war be. Let the drugs be. Let the hate be. Let the punishment be. Let the anxiety be. Let the fear be. Don't explain. Let their expectations be. Kill everything. Kill everyone and let it be. Fuck your sense of hope. And let it be.

Live. Live hopelessly. Die everynight. Die a million times. Die miserably everytime. Die a villian. Die a bad person and die without a cause. Die, lose everything. Then live and lose everything. Embrace a shittier life with open arms. Embrace the fucked up with open arms. Let there be no hope. Hope is a fantasy.

There is a part of me that wants to watch the world burn shamelessly. A place where all the gods will be hopeless. All the heroes will be dead and all hope will be lost. I will be dead somewhere between all this too. I want all of the world to go through the dilemma. All of you shall wonder if you deserve to live. Deserve to make art. Deserve to live. I don't want anarchy. I want hopelessness in each and every brain.

A small part of me wants to watch the world suffer. Suffer from their morals.

I Keep Repeating Rhymes

I keep repeating rhymes
With that one repeating crime.
But I don't contain structure
Not worth a dime.

A poor choice of words
That grotesque pool of tar
Couldn't get me long
But got me out, just far
Enough To waste your time.

I thought my words would rupture
You into bleeding, crying,
Puking, choking, leaving
A never ending scar.
A consciously committed crime.

But I failed
Even before I could hurt you.
The demon inside me bailed
Even before he could see through,

The layers that protected
Your body from me.
He just wasn't strong enough-
Enough to keep you lying.

Why couldn't you lie
to yourself? Was that too
Much to ask from your side?
Could my demons just not be justified?

Perhaps, he never was strong
Enough to waste your time.

So I keep repeating rhymes
With that one repeating crime.

Imagine as vividly as you can and beyond, about all the wrong you can do. About all the ways you can embarrass yourself in front of the most important people in your life. Imagine people who hate you and spite at you and imagine proving them right. Imagine loss of life. Imagine confinement. Imagine all the wasted potential, imagine the dementia, schizophrenia, crimes, torture- both physical and mental, and imagine something 10 times worse. A 100 times worse even. Destroy your brain a little each time you start to imagine.

I imagine the whole world having sex, beating each other, raping each other; they are of all ages and all relations, incestuous even; all relentlessly fucking each other naked; even the dead, even animals, all looking at me, pointing their fingers and laughing at me like maniacs.

They are all moving closer to me. I can smell their saliva, their cum, their shit, their piss, their bile and their blood. All of them rabid, biting each other off. And I imagine all of them pointing at me and say,

"You did this"

As they destroy themselves, only gore remains all around me. My brothers', lovers', father's, haters' and everyone else's blood mixed up and thrown at me to suffocate in.

It is me, just like everything else. I want to see myself punished. I want to feel the pain. I want to this, I want to that, I, I, I…

Fuck me. Kill me. Dont kill me. Cut me up and gut me out. Burn all the veins one by one. Boil my nerves and drill my eye sockets. Saw my bones apart. Do whatever. Just get this out of my head. This toxin. This venom. This demon. Whatever you call it. Cut my legs. Cut my arms. Cut me apart. Blind me. Deafen me. Silent me forever. Do whatever the fuck you want with me.

Take this off me. Take all of this off me. Burn me dead. Burn me to death.

23-10-23

I want to feel something other than guilt. Every human has his share I know. But why does my share suck so much?

If we suck, we suck. If it's good, it's good. If it sucks, it sucks. If we good, we good. If we die, we die. If we live, we live. If we live a half life, we live a half life. If we go to the path of self destruction, we go to the path of self destruction. If we decide to get better, we decide to get better. If we don't, we don't and if we do, we do. There is no surety to any of this.

So why are you afraid of punishment and the lack of?
Why are you afraid of judgement?
There is just no surety.

Lovely, better, hope, good, heal and other words like these. Haven't used them in a while.

To despise oneself so much that words of hope become rare. So rare. Its a real challenge, to survive; and beyond that, self compassion. I look at people who have practiced self compassion and have acceptance; and I wonder how they do it. Will I ever be able to do it?

The answer is always the same,

'Maybe , maybe not.'
Well, guess we will let it be.

Feels so heavy. But I see myself on a cliff. A million people behind me. Teasing me and taunting me. Torturing me with their words.

"Jump, jump, jump… you don't deserve to live you good-for-nothing scum!"

But I'm looking ahead. Listening to each and every word clearly and getting lost in them, I still look ahead. As much true as those people be…

There is a canopy of countless palm tress. They don't
call out my name. But I don't care. I want to
swim in that green water and reach the rock hills
up ahead.
To climb another cliff. To see other people curse
me. To dream of a new canopy.

There is a lot of pent up self hate inside me. Real, desperate, conditional self hate. Real fucking self hate. Self sabotage. Everything is about self. Yeah, it's bleak today.

Rock hills and palm tree canopies? Sucks to not be able to write good sometimes. A lot of self hate. But, gotta live. Live.

A hell lot of self hate. This is going to be a tough task. I am tired of this. Bring back the chaos. Again, I don't know what I'm writing. It's going to be long before I fill this book up.

Another drunk day. Fun ASF trip. No sad RN. a lot more existential than usual.
This feels nice. It feels fun. I'm so creepy this way LMAO.
Every night I stay outside my room to write. Crazy.
It's past 12 at midnight and now I shouldn't stay out. So now I'll stay out. Lmao.

This fucking thing though. I wanna teach EVERYONE how to live; because I myself cannot live. It's a paradox and a meme. I am a MEME.

It's weird because I didn't get blackout kind of drunk but I am drunk enough to feel really good this way. I just wanna keep writing and writing until something good comes up. Which I hardly believe will happen. Man I feel so much sadness. I feel sad as fuck. Another effect of alcohol.

But I am writing. Even though it might be the shittiest thing someone has written; I'm still writing. Like Bukowski. I cannot compare myself to that person but all I know is he's a real writer. I aspire to be a real writer. A real person. I aspire nothing usually; but this I do.

I am willing to accept the misery that will come with these aspirations.

But! Since I have nothing to live for, I gotta go hard. I'll go hard and fast.

Go hard and go fast.

Dude, last night was cool ASF. Gotta stay alive.
Gotta be alive, through bad and worse.
Let's go. One more day.

ONE MORE FREAKING DAY!!!
And then another.
And then another.

Like a hit, a puff that lasts. Let everyday last and help consume the next day. And next, and next, and then next. It's ok to reset. Reset again and again; again, just like a hit.
New born everyday. New born everyday.

Script. Script. Script. OCD. OCD. OCD. Write scripts. Write this. Write that. Write shit. Write. Write. Write. Truth, lies. Good, bad. Nothing fucking works. I'm sick of wanting to be better or being better. I'm sick of thinking I'm not better. That I'm worse. That I'm the worst. I'm bored. I'm sick of judgement. I'm sick of this OCD. Fuck my life. I'm sick of techniques. I'm sick of following a routine. And I'm sick of sleeping in the day. I'm sick of people who pass judgement. I'm sick of people who think they are better just because they think they are. I'm sick of writing. I'm sick of mom's and dad's love and expectations. I'm sick, suicidal and filled with self hatred. I'm sick of people who will laugh at me thinking I complain a lot because I have an easy life. This is just dumb. I'm sick of not being able to treat people nicely. I'm sick of people who think being able to capitalise on everything is life.
I guess I'm just a sick person.

A sick fuck. I'm a sick person. Sitting in front of a reservoir, ducks swimming, followed by the sunset and what do I do?
Eliminate all the good thoughts in my brain one way or another. The grass couldn't be greener and the sun couldnt possibly be any more brighter. It is what it is. But then again, I have all the ugly inside me, the past the present and the future. I have ruined my past and am constantly destroying my present which gets my future in danger.
There is a lot of shit to live for. But how can I? When the brightest of the sun looks as grey as the water down there looks to me; just like everything else. Grey. living for the sake of it.

Fucked past. Fucked up past. I fucked the past up. I, I, I, I…
Ego.

1-11-23

Sad. depressed. Another sad fucking day. Another ramble. Another peak of realisation. Another bout of pure self hate. And another, and another and another. Everyday. I deserve this.

My hands are shaking. The only thing that I'm somewhat good at is gonna be taken away. Shit.

43

1-11-23

Feel it, Sometimes. Sometimes not. I want destruction. Dry up all the beautiful rivers. Fuck all those reflections. Destroy all the rocks, all the mountains and all the shit that is around. Destroy all the guitars, the sketchbooks, the pens, the watercolors. Burn everything. Burn the fucking homes. Burn everyone. Burn fathers, burn mothers, sons, daughters, everyone. Burn me first. Burn me slowly.

A Conversation That Could Be

Hey

"Hey"

So, can I sit here? Around yours?

"Yeah sure, just don't make a mess."

Well, I'll try.

…

So, what's up?

"Nothing. Just, you know, I'm busy"

Yeah. You are.

…

You know? ugh… I don't know what to say or do; or
how to say this. Ask this.

"Wha-"

Like,
Am-am... Am I just always going to be like THIS?

Am I doing something wrong here? Like all the time?
I know, ofcourse I am. But uh, am I uhhhh… completely the wrong one here?

"What exactly are you talking about?"

I'm talking about friendship. About us, yeah. Us.
I mean not necessarily 'Us', but you know… being friends.

Shit. It's embarrassing.
Hey, Do I suck?

"You don't! Well, mostly."

No, nooo, not that way.
But you know? Fuck why am I even asking YOU of all people, about this?

"Now, what is that supposed to mean?"

I'm just a bad person to vibe with. Like I dont suck, man, but I'm not a cheerful person either.
I honestly don't get it man. I'm sorry to bother you with this "monologue". I know it doesn't matter to you. I know I don't.

"It does. You know, you gotta chill dude."

Oh come on now, stop lying. I've noticed the long, slow, awkward pauses we share whenever we look at

each other mid conversation. I'm not a part of your circle either.
And-and I know it's not because I left. It's been this way since we met.

"You're just overthinking. To be blunt, we never really were… pals to begin with."

Ofcourse we weren't! I never asked you that, in a way. I just wanted to be considered. I've always wanted to.
I know when people feel embarrassed of me. Of knowing me.
Like, I'm some kind of abnormal, undercooked french fry between all the normal french fries.
You get it?

"Yeah. GOT. IT."

You know I never wish you or anyone else to be in my shoes. But I just wish you'd know how it feels.
So, where was I?

"French fries?"

Yeah, so… I'm the fry you all will awkwardly look at, then look away; and when all the fries are eaten, most of you will still never consider that weird looking alien of a fry that I am.

Imagine being THAT trash. You will never relate.

"Where are you going with this conversation?"

I don't know.
I'm sorry to bother you. I just wanted to be liked; to be the guy who… was … you know? "chill" to be around. I never got there. For a lot of people I did. But for you, I never could be that person.
I'm sorry to be so irritating to you since we've known each other. I wanted you… to like me. To understand.

"I can still understand. I'll try to-"

But it's too late now. You're not here anymore. Only the things that remind me of you, are here. However much unpleasant those memories of us together are, they… still… are.

"They are..."

Half asleep. On a railway station, I sit with a hoodie and headphones on.
'Good morning, captain' by Slint is playing. Everyone around me is laughing. Having fun. All of them having their moments recorded. And then there's me. Instead of focusing on the present, I am stuck in the future. The future of losing everything I cherish. I will lose. But will I live even after losing everything? Isn't living a human right in itself? I have no strength but I will still live. Live another day. Live another day. More miserable than the one before. And then live another day, more miserable. And then another and another. Maybe. Maybe not. But after today, live another day.

Live another day. And another. And then. Maybe. Decide tomorrow. Let today be. It sucks to be me. My mistakes are a part of my life and I hate myself for that. Mistakes and mistakes and mistakes. OCD. OCD & OCD. it's fucking sad.

I'm really sad today. I can joke around but it's just a distraction. Suicide. Contemplating suicide. But eh. Live another day.
Live another day.

How can I? I have literally told myself a thousand times about how and why I'm the worst person in the world who deserves nothing good. I don't know how much more I can take.

Bouts of anxiety and self doubt. Pills make me feel like I have tourettes. This is not my personal diary but fuck it. Do the impossible. Take the risk of getting love and giving love. For another day. Take the risk. Take risks. Do all the things you believe you don't deserve. You don't deserve ANYTHING, that's good right? Then take a risk for good. Literally. Take the risk for good.

IM SCUM OF SCUM. IM IN A CAFE, WITH A LOT OF CAFFEINE AND CIGARETTES. IM IN THE MOST PRIVILEGED SETTING AND STILL, IM THE SCUM OF THE SCUM.

I MADE A PERSON BEAT THE SHIT OUT OF ME. I FELT NOTHING. I MADE THAT PERSON HURT HIS OWN PARENTS, I FELT NOTHING. I AM READING A BOOK 'MAN'S SEARCH FOR MEANING' AND I FEEL NOTHING. I FELT GUILT FOR TWO YEARS ABOUT MY REAL EVENT. I HAVE REAL EVENT OCD; AND NOW? I FEEL NOTHING. HIGHLY CAFFEINATED. PROZAC AND CLOMIPRAMINE IN MY BODY. IM DONE PRETENDING I LIKE HUMANS. I HATE MYSELF BEYOND REDEMPTION. BEYOND HOPE. THE ONLY MEANING IVE GIVEN TO MY LIFE IS NOW NOT EVEN KNOWN TO ME ANYMORE.

IM SCUM OF THE SCUM.
'GANDI NAALI KA KEEDA' IS AN UNDERSTATEMENT.

I SIT IN A PRIVILEGED SETTING; A CAFE, WITH CIGARETTES AND COFFEE FOR MYSELF. FULL OF STIMULANTS. I AM A ROTTING BODY WITH A NEGATIVELY VALUED SOUL.

TO HAVE ME, YOU PAY A PRICE AND YOUR LIFE WILL ONLY GET WORSE. IM SCUM. I HAVE NO SELF LOVE WHATSOEVER. ITS NOT EVEN OCD AT THIS POINT. IM TOO NAIVE TO LIVE A GOOD LIFE. IM UNDESERVING OF A GOOD LIFE.

BUT ONE THING I MIGHT NOT BE UNDESERVING OF, IS ART. NO ONE CAN STEAL ART FROM ME. NO. ONE. NOT A CAGE. NOT A COFFIN. ILL BLEED WITH MY FINGERS TO MAKE ART. ILL SPIT ON MY BODY TO MAKE ART. ILL CUT MY LIPS AND MAKE ART. BREAK MY TEETH? ILL BREAK MY WHOLE BODY AND MAKE ART.

IM SWEATING AND I DONT FEEL SHIT. A PERSON BEAT ME. MY FACE SHOULD HURT AND IT DOESNT. IM NOT BEYOND UNDERSTANDING THINGS. IVE BECOME MORE NUMB THAN EVER TO UNDERSTAND ANYTHING. THIS FUCKING LIFE IS NOT WORTH FIGHTING FOR. I COULD GET A PANIC ATTACK ANY SECOND AND IT WOULD STILL NOT AFFECT ME. I HAVE STOPPED THE NEED TO BE BETTER. NOTHING WILL MAKE ME REACT NOW. I ATLEAST CRIED AFTER THAT PERSON BEAT ME. NOW I GUESS I WONT EVEN CRY TO A BEATING. ILL PROBABLY CRY, BUT BECAUSE IM SCUM. IM A SKINLESS, SHITLESS TAR FILLED SCUM WHO SWEATS NEGATIVITY AND REEKS OF PATHETICNESS.

NOTHING CAN HELP ME. DONT EVEN WANT TO BE PROVED WRONG ANYMORE.
I MIGHT FAINT. I WILL. NONE OF IT MAKES SENSE TO ME. NOT DEEP, NOT ALISHA, NOT VISHAL, NOT JAY, NOT MY BROTHERS, NOT HARSHIL, NOT MY SISTERS, NOT MY MAASIS, NOT MY GRANDMAS NOT MY PARENTS EVEN.

I SEE NO POINT TO PROVE. I SEE NOTHING TO PROVE. I JUST WANT TO SUFFER MORE AND MORE.
FUCK MY LIFE.

EVERYTIME I WRITE 'I HATE MYSELF', IT FEELS JUST AS TRUE AS THE LAST TIME, IF NOT MORE. IM LYING, IT IS MORE.

NOTHING IS GOING TO STOP ME. I WANT TO BURN EVERYTHING THAT RELATES TO ME. ANYTHING THAT SHOWS OF ME, I WANT TO BURN. ITS NOT MY PARENTS. THEY DONT SHOW OF WHAT I AM. PEOPLE IM ASSOCIATED WITH, DONT SHOW OF WHAT I AM. MY BROTHER DOESNT SHOW OF WHAT I AM. NO.

ITS THIS DIARY, THIS PEN, THAT GUITAR AND MY ART THAT SHOWS OF WHAT I AM. WHEN I DIE. BURN THIS BOOK. BURN ALL THE BOOKS AND ALL THE SKETCHES.

NOTHING THAT SHOWS OF ME SHALL REMAIN.

ONLY THE IDEAS OF ME, THAT THE PEOPLE HAVE, GOOD OR BAD; SHALL CONTINUE AS THEY NATURALLY HAVE TO.

THIS COULD VERY WELL BE THE END. AND THIS IS NOT TO COPY KAFKA OR COBAIN, OR HUNTER S THOMPSON OR ANYONE ELSE. THIS IS ME. DONT MAKE ME LIVE LONG. DONT MAKE SOMETHING OUT OF ME WHICH ISNT. THIS IS ME. SHIT. A NUMB SMELLY SHIT.

What is the end goal here? Do I write to relate to other people if I can't even help myself anymore? I cannot even empathize with myself anymore.

HOW WILL I HELP OTHER PEOPLE THEN? I GUESS WE'LL FIND OUT. BECAUSE THAT'S THE END GOAL RIGHT?

THAT? IT MUST BE SOMETHING ELSE. AGAIN I DON'T 100% KNOW IF THERE IS AN END GOAL, BUT I GOTTA WRITE. TAKE THE RISK OF WRITING. THE ONE THING I WANT MY OCD TO NOT ATTACK.

SO I CAN HELP SOMEONE OUT OF THIS SELF HATE. HELP SOMEONE. WISH I COULD WRITE MORE THAN THIS.

What will I be remembered for?
If someone reads this diary, I might be remembered for the irrational self hate and critical judgement I gave to myself. Or am I really a bad person?
Will I be remembered for the little good I did? Will I be remembered for the little shit I was? I just don't know the answer.
Everyday I remind myself that it's okay to not know. I don't know who I am. I don't know what I am. I wanna cry all the time. I just wanna cry all the time. I want to cry. I need to cry. Let me cry.

6-12-23

Waiting for my head to blow up. Need it to blow the hell up. Too much baggage. Head hurts. It pains. A lot of pain.
Dumb. Fucked. Weird. Gotta get this shit off me. This is how I write now. Like a bitch. I write shit not worth reading anymore. Shit is not worth writing anymore too. Again, not romanticising. I just am bored and I'd rather waste my time writing this fuckery than write anything meaningful or do anything meaningful.

I don't know metaphors. I don't know vocabulary. I'm not a fucking poet. Worse, I'm a writer, a very shit one.

Me, me this, I'm this, I'm that. Fucking self obsessed half ass piece of self loathing shit. And I write this on display. FFS. no hope. Shit.

Nobody knows one thing about me. Today is a shit day. I'll nap. I wanna nap. I feel shit. Shit day. Wanna cry. Don't wanna write anymore at the moment. Head pains. It pains.
Shit. Scum. Garbage. Weirdass vocabulary. Not punk. Just shit. Smelly fucked up, punched in, dived in hump of shit.
Eh. bored. OCD attacks are back. No strength. Shit day.

Suicidal. Everything else is just a bonus.

The hate is bonus. The music is bonus. The betrayal is bonus. The work is bonus. The hatred is bonus. The headache is bonus. The pain is bonus. The attention seeking is bonus. The nail paint is bonus. The jittery hand is bonus. The pills are bonus.
The life, that sucks, is bonus.
 :(is bonus. Art is bonus.

9-12-23

And I wanna write. Write more and then some. I want my head to burst open and get empty. Ruined. Dead piece of shit. I gotta end up dead and fucked. I'm gonna. This is an unhealthy thought. I'm an unhealthy human. Fucking sucks. I'm losing my mind. I'm losing everything. I, myself, am losing. I'm wasting myself away. I'm wasting myself away. I'm wasting life. I'm a wasted person. I'm wasted. Rape me. Rape me. Torture me. Kill me and fuck me. Fuck and kill me. Just do something to me. Make something out of me.

It's high time I publish a book. I don't know if I want to. But if I do, this is probably gonna be the last entry of my book.

I am afraid of not knowing anything and it has driven my mind to sadness. If someone has read all of this, my world may fall apart. My parents may hate me for everything.

My ambitions of helping someone with mental health issues might come true. My fears of comments of my seniors and elders might come true. OR they might support me. I might keep wondering what I am and never know the answer.

Am I bad? Am I good? Am I an ace? What is my identity? Will I this? Will I that? And an endless cycle of questions.

Will I know all the answers? Is it my job to know all the answers? I dont know.

The end of this book is a beginning to a conversation I'm probably not ready to have.

Do you have a meaningless life?
Do you ridicule meaningless lives?
Or are you somewhere in between?

I'm the worst of both worlds.

They adore me and I hate myself. They hate me enough to not talk to me and I love myself enough to try and keep living everyday.

Pent up anger inside me. I don't want the world to feel good about itself. They end up hating me. That's my punishment. I hate me.

Something has convinced me that I'm not allowed to live a normal life. When I'm too conscious of my thoughts, they turn to rape, murder, misery, birth, death, destruction, mutilation, bloodbath, art and everything in between. It doesn't just end there, it imagines a combination of possibilities and then their combinations and then both the extreme polars of the final, already ambiguous result.

I am both the nicest human in the world and the worst possible thing who wants to hurt the whole mankind. It's not just my trauma, my pent up anger or my loneliness or my lack of feelings or my bipolarity or my ocd or anything else. It's myself.

I don't even want the world to know what my mind imagines and I also want everyone of you to taste this shit if you already don't. I assume you do relate. I wanna punish you more.

15-12-23

There is always someone in the world who wants someone to feel bad about themselves.

It's an impulse. And I like the idea of that impulse. Even if it arises for a millisecond.

Even if it is not considered, observed or acknowledged. But the impulse to let go; Let go of the idea, of thoughts, the ideas of attraction and repulsion, the ideas of freedom and confinement. Just let go. Pure, inexplicable impulse.

Its a rather boring attempt to get off the fucking cigarettes and to impress people and to be righteous. I am getting bored of the ideas that I've had about people, about rights, about teachers, about everything. It's a big transitional period in my life and I feel tired to react. I feel tired to react and I feel tired to act. I have started letting go and I really don't know what to do with this information.

It really sucks to want to react but not have the energy to. I really don't have the energy to react to half of the things you are saying.

And I know it might hurt you to know this but I really have become indifferent to a lot of things that I thought I cared about. I wish I was affected by the lot of you. But I don't understand the duality that you guys have to offer.

I want to be done being likeable and being dislikeable for I don't really understand what you want from me anymore and I also don't understand if

I want to give you the liberty to get what you want from me.

If I am bad, then why do I really need to react to your ideas of good? Why do I need to react to my ideas of good? I don't know what I'm going through. I could really fucking blast myself out on you people but would it really matter?

I don't really understand you people. You want to shut me up. You want me to speak. What the fuck do I owe you? What?

I'd rather fucking do if you stop disturbing me and get what you want, quietly, peacefully out of me. But you'd rather hurt me and expect me to hurt you. Nope. I don't do that. I disregard your thoughts today. I will be selfish. For you are selfish. I avoid what you are altogether. And I'll avoid myself too. I'd like that.

Why today?

Well today because I contain the power to destroy other things by my words. I put out the worst in everybody sometimes. I hate myself for it. I hate myself for making myself your duty. I hate myself for making you believe that you have something to do with my destruction. I hate myself for giving you that idea.

I hate myself for having the idea of inaction. It all builds up, the idea of inaction; and keeps building up and building up until I do something that is extraordinarily damaging. I can't stop being myself and I hate myself for that.

I am so, so done with myself. Not you guys. It's not your fault that I'm like this. I decided to contain all the fucked up shit for these 22 years and contain some more. You believe it is your duty to treat me like I'm a patient. But I give up being a patient. I give up being an experiment for myself and for others. I give up.

And I want to give up all the ideas that I have about myself. That I am something. That I am special and that the world is unfair. I want to give all these ideas up. But I just can't seem to. I always end up agreeing with people about the notion that I CAN be nice, that I AM allowed to live, that the world IS unfair and it is also fair sometimes. That I can be unfair too.

I want to give all these ideas up that I have built up for myself and for you. It's not a competition. I don't want it to be a competition. I don't want you to think that leaving me alone makes you 'win' over me. I don't want to 'win' over you. I don't want to 'lose' from you.

I want to be free. Free from all this literature and psychological mambo jumbo that I have fed myself. I want to but I somehow fail to have these things many times. So I'm done. I'm tired and I don't know if it gets worse or better. I don't want to care if it gets worse or better. I don't know where peace comes from. I don't even know if I want it anymore.

I will be called off as a crazy person if someone reads this after I'm dead. I'll be called different. I don't want to call myself anything. And yet, I still fail at all these ambitions.

So why not suicide?
Why even suicide?
Why not just give the fuck up?

River

I wish we never met.

I wish, that you weren't looking down at me with those grey eyes. They looked cold the very moment before we touched each other. I could see the pupils screaming a thousand thoughts about a thousand people and choosing to look at me with all that rage. Maybe it was never my call. But the moment you looked at me after you walked up that bridge, I wished you were a hallucination.

I wished that you would come down to me, move me with your tender feet, talk to me, do anything at all, to find my reality out. I hoped for you to know, that I would burn your lungs out and break your body down to nothing, very very slowly, before granting the liberty you seeked inside me.

I wish you knew, that us crashing had changed the very course of the world in a manner only you would understand.

I'm still flowing, carrying you and a lot others, accepting you all as you are and becoming, when those up there couldn't.